DATE DUE

· THE · ZABAJABA JUNGLE

WILLIAM STEIG

MICHAEL DI CAPUA BOOKS

FARRAR · STRAUS · GIROUX NEW YORK

TO AURORA

Library of Congress catalog card number: 87-17690
Published simultaneously in Canada by Collins Publishers, Toronto
Color separations by Offset Separations Corp.
Printed and bound in the United States of America
by Horowitz/Rae Book Manufacturers
Designed by Atha Tehon
First edition, 1987

Leonard is slashing at the vines and creepers with his sharp bolo. He is fighting his way into the Zabajaba Jungle, where, it is said, no human being has ever penetrated.

Why is he there? He himself doesn't know. He just has to push on.

One more whack and he breaks through. Squawking birds and raucous insects fly about. Some sit in trees, staring.

A hungry plant gropes for him, but he jumps away. He'd better keep a grip on his bolo!

What's this? A big butterfly in the jaws of a flower! Leonard strikes, again and again, until it lets go. The butterfly takes off.

Steaming rain falls, Leonard walks faster. What now? The gaping mouth of a petrified monster!

He steps inside, crawls through the gullet, and enters the belly. Behold! There is strange writing on the wall. So others *were* here before him.

Leonard explores the intestines, where prickly creatures scurry, brushing against his legs. At last he sees daylight and exits through the great cloaca.

Now the jungle is dim and hushed. It's getting late, and all that green makes him sleepy.

He rigs up his hammock and falls into it.

Night comes, and he has doubts about the dark. Who's out there? When he flashes on his light, all he sees is what he saw before — the vegetable universe.

He stretches out again. Then Leonard and his light go off together.

When he wakes up, the ground is covered with a writhing, hissing mesh of snakes. Leonard wishes he was home in bed.

But look! It's the big butterfly, hovering by the hammock! He mounts its furry back and is lifted away.

The butterfly carries him to a glade of flowers and flutters off.

There is birdsong, and then a voice calling: “Oh, human being!”

“Who’s that?” he asks.
“I’m Flora.”
“I’m Leonard,” says Leonard. “Come out and let me see you.”

"I can't. I'm too shy. But listen, Leonard. Those yellow flowers over there are full of delectable nectar. Just help yourself."

"Thank you," says Leonard.

"My pleasure," says Flora. "Farewell!" Leonard gets a glimpse of an ungainly bird hopping off through the trees.

He climbs into the bowl of a yellow flower and tastes the nectar. How strange! Somehow he always knew this special sweetness existed.

But what on earth? The flower is suddenly rising! He'd better jump. Now!

Is this the last of Leonard? No. His fall is broken by tiers of fern fronds.

A bunch of mandrills with blue behinds is waiting down below. They drag him off.

They come to a deep hole in the ground, toss him in, and leave. Leonard keeps trying to hack out steps with his bolo. No use.

During the night, the mandrills return and let down a rope ladder. Leonard scrambles up, right into their arms.

They bring him before three judges, one with a bird head, one with a rat head, and one with the head of a snake.

"Person," asks Birdhead, "what are you doing in the Zabajaba Jungle?"

"I don't really know."

"Who told you you could drink the nectar of the Jabazaba Flower?" asks Rathead.

"A funny-looking bird."

"Aha, that impossible Flora!" says Snakehead. "It so happens it's against the law to even take a sip of Jabazaba nectar. Who do you think you are?"

"Leonard!" cries a voice from the bushes. "Show them who you are! Do your stuff."

Leonard takes some fireworks out of his knapsack and sets off an awesome display. His captors are transfixed.

Flora leaps out. "Hurry, Leonard! This way!" They hasten down a secret path. At the end of it, she says, "Farewell, brave boy, farewell!"

Leonard clambers over some rocks and is surprised to see an enormous bottle with his parents inside. He taps on the glass, but they don't look up. He bangs with his bolo. They still don't hear him.

He finds a rock and smashes a hole in the bottle. Now they see him! They rush out with embraces and kisses for their beloved son.

Leonard is pleased.

"Where are we?" his father asks.
"In the Zabajaba Jungle."
"How do we get out?"
"Follow me," says Leonard.